THIS ·GRETCHEN· BOOK

BELONGS TO:

To our parents
AJH
BJS

GRETCHEN'S WORLD™

illustrated by:
BARBI SARGENT

written by:
ALICE HOFFER

ART DIRECTION BY DICK CHIARA

Library of Congress Catalog Card Number: 80-83354. ISBN: 0-448-16560-0 (Trade Edition). Copyright © 1981 by American Greetings Corp.
All rights reserved. Published simultaneously in Canada. Printed in the United States of America.

Publishers • GROSSET & DUNLAP • New York
A FILMWAYS COMPANY

What's the matter, little girl?"

A cheerful voice startled Gretchen. On the soft, green grass near her hand sat a beautiful bluebird.

"I'm just not very happy today," Gretchen answered.

"But it's much too lovely a day to be sad!" the bluebird said. "My bird friends and I have been singing from the treetops since early this morning!"

As she listened, a big, wet tear rolled down the girl's cheek.

"You must be new around here! My name's Barnabas."

"I'm Gretchen," she said, wiping her tears on her sleeve. "And when you said the word 'friends,' I was thinking of all the ones I left behind. Now I have no one to play with!"

"There, there," comforted the bird, "we will just have to find some friends for you."

She brightened. "Can we start now?"

"Start what?" asked the bird.

"Start finding me some friends!"

"Pity, pity," he shrugged. "The only friends I have are other birds. You can't very well play with them unless you can fly. But I know someone we could ask about this. Come along."

So off they went through the meadow, across the slippery rocks in the bubbly creek, and over the hill to the brick alley at the edge of town, where four cats sprawled lazily.

"Hello, Chester," called the bird.

"Well, curl my whiskers, if it isn't Barnabas Bluebird," grinned the cat.

"This is Gretchen," Barnabas said. "We want to talk to you."

"Delighted," exclaimed Chester. "It isn't often I get company! What can I do for you?"

"Gretchen's new in the neighborhood," Barnabas said, "and she doesn't have any friends to play with. I thought you might be able to help us."

The wise old cat scratched the back of his ear while he thought very hard.

"I've got it," he shouted suddenly. "The answer is—FIND her some friends!" And with that, he began to purr loudly, feeling very pleased with himself.

"We already know THAT!" cried Barnabas. "We hoped you could tell us HOW she can find some!"

Chester let out a rather forlorn meow.

"The only friends I have are other cats," he replied, "and they wouldn't be much help. She probably doesn't even like catnip."

"Well, there must be something we can do," sighed the bird.

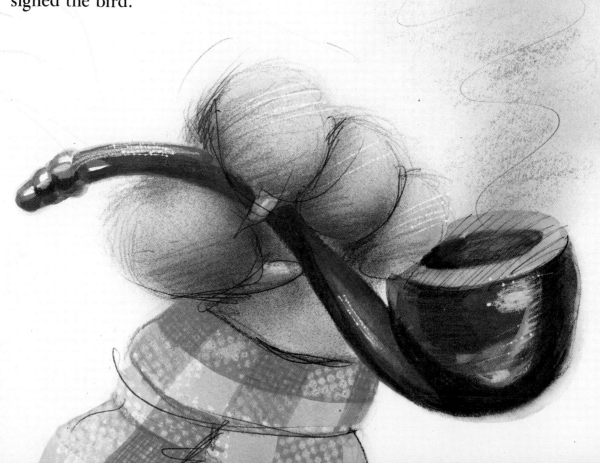

"Of course!" Chester said as he jumped to his feet. "Follow me! If there's anyone who knows how to find friends, it's Penelope."

They all ran out of the alley, and down the hill to the edge of the bubbly creek. When they reached the fallen oak, Chester stopped and whistled.

SMACK! came a reply from the water behind the tree. SMACKA-WHACKY-SMAT!

"Howdy-dooooooooo," meowed Chester.

WHACKY-WHOOSH, and WHACKY-WHOOSH, SMACKY-WHOOSH! came the sounds. A pointed brown snout popped out of the water. And following the snout came two round black eyes, two tiny brown ears, and a very round belly. And then Gretchen saw a larger and grander tail than she ever imagined.

"Howdy-do!" said Penelope Beaver, as she dripped water all over the ground. "A pleasant surprise, indeed!" and she wiggled her nose at them.

"Gretchen and Barnabas, meet Penelope," said the cat. "We came to ask you a very important question."

"Oh, how exciting," exclaimed the beaver. "But first let us have a snack."

Penelope led them to a clearing by a tall elm. She spread out a red checkered kerchief on an old stump and brought out her best china cups. While water for tea boiled in the sun, she put strawberries on the table. When the tea was poured, Penelope was ready to talk.

"Now, Chester, WHAT is this terribly important question? I'll bet it has something to do with your new friend."

They all looked at Gretchen, who was slowly sipping her tea and staring unhappily into the woods.

"Well," said Barnabas, taking over the conversation, "I found Gretchen crying in the meadow this morning because she doesn't have any friends to play with. Our terribly important question is, 'What do you think she should do?'"

"Indeed!" replied the beaver. "I've never had this problem myself. I have many friends, but I doubt they would make good playmates for Gretchen. She doesn't have large front teeth for chipping wood, and she certainly couldn't WHACKY-WHOOSH without a tail! However, I DO think I may have an answer."

The three looked eagerly at the fat little beaver.

"She should FIND some friends!" And at that, Penelope's tail clapped and slapped in happiness.

"Please stop slapping the ground," Chester pleaded. "We haven't solved anything, and I'm getting a headache!"

"That noise is not from my tail," said Penelope.

At that moment, they heard a distant sound like the rumbling of thunder from the far edge of the woods. The birds stopped singing in the treetops, and the squirrels froze in their tracks. Penelope's teacups began to rattle in their saucers.

"What is that?" Gretchen gasped, her eyes growing wide at the sound.

"Why, that's IT!" exclaimed Penelope. "Now I know who we can ask! Follow me."

They ran through the woods, and the thundering sound grew louder and louder. Suddenly, Penelope skidded to a stop and motioned for them to follow very slowly.

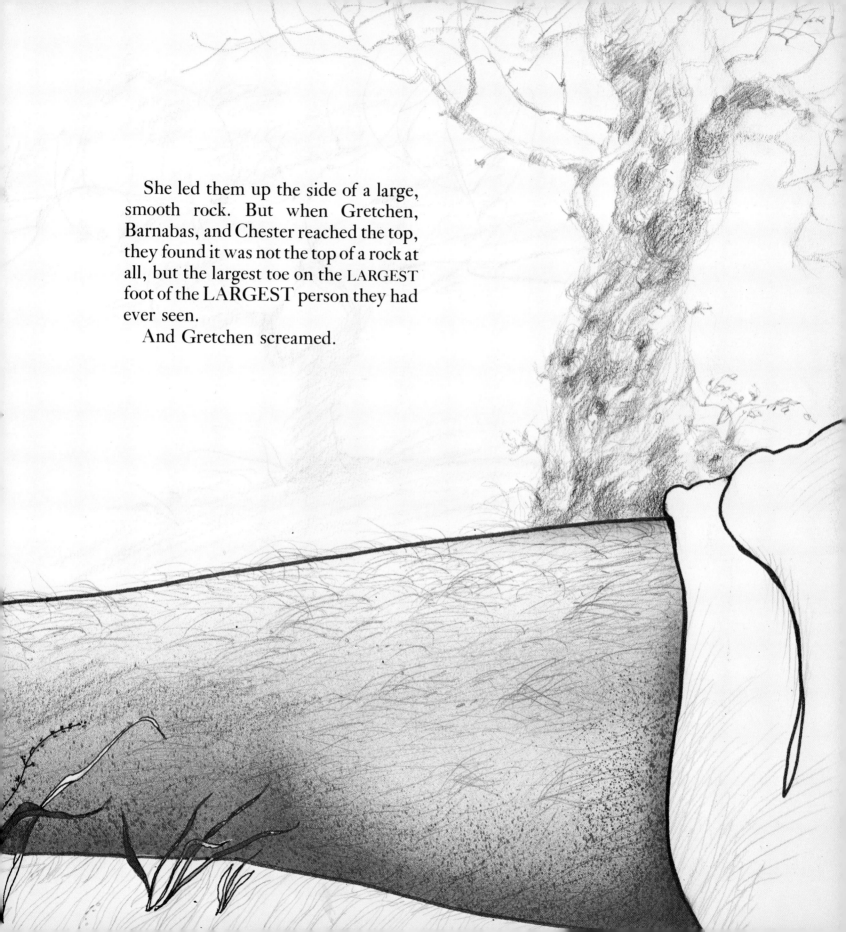

She led them up the side of a large, smooth rock. But when Gretchen, Barnabas, and Chester reached the top, they found it was not the top of a rock at all, but the largest toe on the LARGEST foot of the LARGEST person they had ever seen.

And Gretchen screamed.

The giant's eyes popped open, and he looked down at them. Gretchen, Barnabas, and Chester tried to hide behind his toes, hoping not to be noticed. But the beaver was not afraid. She just scrambled right up onto the giant's knee.

"Hello, Penelope Beaver," boomed the giant. "I thought I heard someone call. Was I snoring very loudly and rattling your teacups again?"

"Howdy-do, Gargantuan," Penelope called. "That's not why we came. I do apologize for waking you, but we have a terribly important question to ask."

"You needn't be afraid of me," the giant said as he reached out a large but gentle hand to pick up Penelope, Gretchen, Barnabas, and Chester. The giant's smile was big and bright, and his voice was kind. They all felt better instantly.

Penelope began to explain their problem, and the wise old giant listened carefully. When the story was finished, he placed them back on the ground nearby. He took a golden flute from his pocket and began to play a melody. Soon they were surrounded by beautiful fairies and woodland sprites, tiny gnomes, and several important-looking trolls.

"All this looks VERY exceptional!" Penelope whispered to herself.

"It must be a matter of great importance for you to call us in the middle of the afternoon," said a sprite.

"Indeed, it is," Gargantuan agreed, and he explained the problem. When he had finished, one of the fairies asked, "Would it be helpful if we all told Gretchen how we made our friends?"

"Yes," said Gargantuan. "Let's *DO* that! Who will begin?"

Barnabas was first to speak. "I remember that I chirped a lot and sang happy songs throughout the day. That always seemed to bring new friends my way!"

There was cheering from the sprites.

Chester followed. "I play games a lot," he said, "and I've found I make friends by taking turns."

"Wonderful," exclaimed the giant, as the gnomes applauded. He turned to Penelope. "How about you?" he asked.

"We can tell you about her," called a tiny voice. It was Aurora, the queen of all the magical creatures. The little beaver looked down at her feet shyly.

"Penelope is the friendliest of all," she continued. "She shares her tea with everyone, and we hear her happy 'Howdy-do' echoing through the trees all day."

Gargantuan looked at Gretchen and saw that she was beginning to understand the special secrets of friendship.

"If you remember what you have heard here," promised Gargantuan, "you shall soon have many new friends of your own."

Then the fairies began to dance, and the gnomes and trolls clapped a rhythmic beat. The meadow sprites twirled and circled overhead and made a beautiful rainbow of color.

Suddenly Gretchen awoke with a start. Standing on the hillside right next to her was a boy with a round straw hat.

"You were asleep," he said.

"But, where are Chester and Penelope and . . ."

"I don't know who they are, but I'm Charlie. And YOU must be Gretchen."

She blinked and rubbed her sleepy eyes. "How did you know that?"

"A little bird told me!" he said. "And I came to tell you that all my friends are going to the meadow for a picnic. Would you like to come along?"

Gretchen smiled her brightest smile. She thought of the secrets that Barnabas, Chester, and Penelope had shared with her. And she could almost hear Gargantuan as he said, *"If you remember what you have heard here, you shall soon have many friends of your own."*

Gretchen whispered as she ran down to the meadow, "Thank you, Gargantuan, I'll never forget!"

And she never did.